CLEMENTINE ROSE

and the Perfect Present

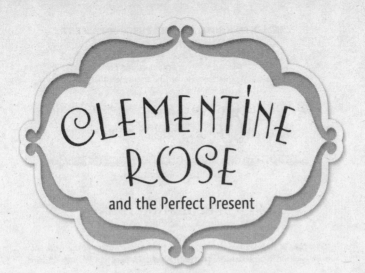

CLEMENTINE ROSE
and the Perfect Present

Jacqueline Harvey

RED FOX

CLEMENTINE ROSE AND THE PERFECT PRESENT
A RED FOX BOOK 978 1 849 41873 7

Published in Great Britain by Red Fox,
an imprint of Random House Children's Publishers UK
A Random House Group Company

Penguin
Random House
UK

Originally published in Australia by Random House Australia in 2013
This edition published 2014

1 3 5 7 9 10 8 6 4 2

Text copyright © Jacqueline Harvey, 2013

The Random House Group Limited supports the Forest Stewardship Council (FSC®),
the leading international forest certification organisation. Our books carrying the
FSC label are printed on FSC®-certified paper. FSC is the only forest certification
scheme supported by the leading environmental organisations, including Greenpeace.
Our paper procurement policy can be found at www.**randomhouse**.co.uk/environment.

Set in ITC Century

RANDOM HOUSE CHILDREN'S PUBLISHERS UK
61–63 Uxbridge Road, London W5 5SA

www.**randomhousechildrens**.co.uk
www.**totallyrandombooks**.co.uk
www.**randomhouse**.co.uk

Addresses for companies within The Random House Group Limited
can be found at: www.**randomhouse**.co.uk/offices.htm

THE RANDOM HOUSE GROUP Limited Reg. No. 954009

A CIP catalogue record for this book is available from the British Library.

Printed and bound in Great Britain by
CPI Group (UK) Ltd, Croydon, CR0 4YY

*For Ian, who is with me every step of
the way, and for Chris and Kimberley and
Anne, who work so hard to bring
it all together.*

THE
INVITATION

Clementine Rose stood on her tippy-
toes with her arms around her
mother's waist. The woman leaned
down and kissed the top of the child's golden
head.

'Have a wonderful day,' Lady Clarissa said to
her daughter.

'I will.' Clemmie let go and ran to the basket
near the stove where Lavender, her teacup
pig, and Pharaoh, Aunt Violet's sphynx cat, were
snuggled together. She knelt down and pressed

1

her face between them. Pharaoh's sandpaper tongue shot out and licked Clementine's cheek.

'That tickles, Pharaoh,' she giggled.

Lavender grunted, then closed her eyes and went back to sleep.

'Run along, Clemmie. You don't want to keep Uncle Digby waiting,' her mother instructed, then turned and headed up the back stairs. She was on her way to check that all of the bedrooms were made up, ready for the full house they were expecting on the weekend. It would be the first time since Lady Clarissa had opened Penberthy House to paying guests that every single room was booked.

Clementine wriggled into her coat and threw her backpack on her shoulders. 'Bye Mummy.' She sped towards the entrance hall.

She glanced up at the portraits of her grandparents on the wall as she flung open the front door. 'By Granny and Grandpa.'

Clementine hadn't noticed Aunt Violet standing on the third-floor landing.

'Does she really think you could care less,

Edmund?' the woman said as she peered at the painting of her brother. She didn't hear Lady Clarissa approach.

'Who are you talking to, Aunt Violet?' asked the younger woman.

'No one!' Aunt Violet snapped. 'You must be hearing things, Clarissa.'

Her niece grinned. 'Has Clementine got you talking to the relatives too?'

'Oh, don't be ridiculous. The child clearly lives in fairyland,' Aunt Violet said with a huff. 'I was not talking to my brother or anyone else, for that matter.'

'Well, there's no harm in it, I'm sure,' Clarissa replied. 'Clementine seems to get on rather well with all of them.'

'What a load of tripe.' Violet harrumphed and strode off towards the bathroom.

Meanwhile, Clementine Rose had met Uncle Digby and clambered into the car. The pair chatted away as they always did on the short run from Penberthy Floss to the school in Highton Mill.

The little car sputtered down the lane, which was lined on both sides by low stone walls. They soon stopped outside Ellery Prep's ornate gates and pretty hedge. Clementine leaned through the gap in the seats and kissed Uncle Digby's cheek.

He turned and grinned at her. 'Have a good day, Clemmie.'

'I will.' She hopped out of the car and ran to join Sophie, who had just arrived too.

Uncle Digby rolled down the top of his window. 'Good morning, Pierre.' His warm breath fogged up the cold glass as he called to Sophie's father, whose van was idling on the other side of the road.

'Good morning, Monsieur Digby. Please tell Lady Clarissa that the cake is almost finished and it looks beautiful.' He squeezed his forefinger and thumb together and kissed them.

'Good job, Pierre. I might pop around to the shop and have a quick look.' Uncle Digby winked. 'Just so I can put her mind at ease and let her know that it's perfect.'

'Ah, I think the cream buns will be ready too,' Pierre replied. 'I have some deliveries to make but Odette is there.'

Digby waved goodbye and eased the little car onto the road. He could have walked the short distance to the shop but the wind was chilly and he hadn't been feeling quite himself the past couple of days. He didn't want to get sick before the weekend. Lady Clarissa would have too many guests to manage without his help.

Clementine and Sophie bounded across the playground and straight to the classroom to drop off their bags. Poppy was already there talking with Astrid, the cleverest girl in the class. If anyone could be relied upon to know the answer to a difficult question it was her.

The girls greeted one another and decided to play hopscotch before the bell.

'Are you going to Angus's party?' Poppy asked the group as she threw a cold stone onto the asphalt.

Sophie and Astrid nodded. Clementine's

tummy twinged and she wondered what they were talking about.

'I don't really want to but Mummy says that it's unkind not to go, especially since he wrote the invitation himself and even put it in the mail,' Sophie explained. 'What about you, Clementine?'

'I didn't get invited,' she replied, frowning.

'Maybe the postman is running late at your house. My invitation only came yesterday,' Astrid offered.

Clementine nodded. That seemed reasonable enough. They didn't have the mail delivered every day. Her mother or Uncle Digby had to go to Mrs Mogg's store to collect it.

Angus and Joshua raced past the girls.

'You'd better get me good presents,' Angus called. 'Otherwise I'll tie you up and feed you to the dragon.'

'Yeah, you'd better,' Joshua yelled. 'His dragon is really mean.'

Clementine wrinkled her nose. 'I bet his dragon is bossy too, just like him and his Nan.'

Sophie looked at Clementine and coughed loudly.

Mrs Bottomley was standing right behind the group. 'What was that, young lady?'

The child spun around.

'Nothing, Mrs Bottomley,' Clementine lied. As the teacher also happened to be Angus's nan, Clementine hoped she hadn't heard her.

'I'll have you know that my daughter is going to a lot of trouble for this party. Even though I told her it was a ridiculous idea to have it after school, when the children will be tired and grumpy. I've been asked to make the cake, which I trust will not be eaten by some ghastly cat this time.' Mrs Bottomley was referring to the last sponge cake she'd made, which had been nibbled by Aunt Violet's cat, Pharaoh, at the pet day and then completely ruined when Mrs Bottomley fell into it. 'I suggested that she leave some of the students who might not be able to behave themselves properly off the guest list.'

Mrs Bottomley arched her eyebrow at Clementine and walked away.

Clementine felt another twinge in her tummy. What if she really wasn't invited? Did Mrs Bottomley think she couldn't be trusted at a birthday party? That wasn't true at all. There were plenty of other kids in the class who were naughty – Joshua, for a start. He was always in trouble, especially with Miss Critchley, the head teacher.

Sophie pulled a face. 'She's so mean.'

'Don't worry, Clementine. If you're not invited I'll tell Mummy I don't want to go either,' Poppy said.

'I don't want to go to Angus's stupid party anyway,' Clementine declared.

But that wasn't true at all. By morning tea time Clementine had learned that the whole class had been invited. Every – single – one. Except her. There was even a dress-up theme: kings and queens, princes and princesses. Angus said that he was only having the queens and princesses so that the kings and princes could capture them and feed them to the dragon that lived in the cave at the bottom of his garden. Astrid said that was rubbish because everyone knew dragons weren't real. Clementine wasn't so sure but she hoped Astrid was right.

Clementine loved to dress up. She even had the perfect outfit, which Mrs Mogg had made for Clemmie's own princess party the year before. It was a pink gown with lace, and a hooped skirt underneath to make it stick out, just like a proper princess dress. She had a silver tiara with pink stones in it and her mother had found a long pearl necklace and a pearl bracelet in one of the trunks in the attic. Deep down, Clementine hoped that when she got home that afternoon, the invitation had arrived.

LEFT OUT

'Angus is having a party, Mummy,' Clementine told her mother when Lady Clarissa picked her up from school.

'That's nice, Clemmie,' her mother replied distantly. She was mentally checking off some of the jobs she still had to get done before the weekend.

'Everyone's invited –' Clementine began.

'That's very kind of Mr and Mrs Archibald.'

'– except me,' Clementine finished sulkily.

'Oh dear, that's no good,' said Lady Clarissa. She glanced between the road and Clemmie's crestfallen reflection in the rear-vision mirror.

'Were there any letters today?' Clemmie asked hopefully.

'Not that I remember, darling. But we can check when we get home. When's the party?'

'After school on Tuesday. But I don't care.' Clementine wiped a hand across her eye. 'Angus is horrible.'

'I thought you were getting on better with him,' her mother said calmly.

Clementine shrugged. 'Mrs Bottomley said that she told Angus's mum not to invite any troublemakers and then she looked straight at *me*.'

'Never mind, Clemmie. I could phone Angus's mother and see if there's been a mistake, if you like,' Lady Clarissa suggested.

'No! Then he'll just say that I'm a crybaby. I don't want to go.'

'If that's how you really feel, I'm happy not to interfere. There's so much to do at home

and I certainly need your help this weekend.'
Lady Clarissa smiled in the rear-vision mirror.
'Poor Uncle Digby is run off his feet and Aunt
Violet's being her usual unhelpful self.'

Clementine decided not to think about
Angus and his party again. There were much
more interesting things going on at home.

When her mother first told her there was
to be a wedding at the house, Clementine had
been bursting with excitement. She couldn't
stop talking about it. She'd never been to a
wedding before.

'But where will everyone sit?' Clementine
had asked her mother at the time. Penberthy
House was big but the dining room could fit
only twenty people at the most.

'We're going to put a tent in the back garden,'
her mother had explained.

'A tent? But that's even smaller than the
dining room.' Clementine wondered if the
people getting married were tiny, like pixies
or elves.

'Oh no, Clemmie, this tent will be enormous,' her mother had reassured her.

'Like the circus?' Clementine had asked. Her mother and Uncle Digby had taken Clemmie to the circus the last time it came to the showground at Highton Mill.

'A little bit like that,' her mother had replied.

'But without the elephants or the lions,' Clementine decided.

It had all seemed so far away when her mother first mentioned it. It was before Aunt Violet had come to stay and before Clemmie had started school. And now there was only one more day until the men would come and put up the tent and then the guests would begin to arrive. Every room had been booked by the wedding party and their families.

Lady Clarissa turned into the driveway and Clementine spotted Mrs Mogg's car parked next to Uncle Digby's.

'Oh, that's a relief,' Lady Clarissa exhaled. 'Margaret said she'd pop over and help Uncle Digby with some of the cleaning this afternoon.'

Clementine thought she could ask Mrs Mogg if she'd brought any letters too. She didn't *really* care about Angus and his party, of course. But she'd check anyway, just to be sure.

A BIG TENT
FOR A BIG DAY

On Saturday morning, Clementine Rose sat on the back steps of the house. She was watching the men hammering a line of long metal spikes into the ground. A large sheet of canvas was spread across the lawn like a giant white blanket. She couldn't wait to see it transform into the tent. Lavender was sitting beside her, dozing in the wintry sun. Both girl and pig were wearing matching pretty blue jumpers, which Mrs Mogg had knitted a few weeks earlier.

Friday at school had been awful. Everyone had been talking about their costumes for Angus's party and Angus had demanded all sorts of presents. Clementine's invitation had never arrived, so she decided that she would just ignore the other kids and think about what was happening at home.

But a sick feeling returned to the bottom of her tummy whenever anyone mentioned it. Even Angus had asked her about his present. She definitely wasn't getting him anything if she wasn't invited.

The weather had turned much colder in the past few days, and with the last autumn leaves scattered across the ground, Clementine thought the garden looked a bit sad and scruffy. She wondered if the tent would be warm enough, but her mother had assured her that this wouldn't be any ordinary construction. Clementine thought it was looking a lot bigger than the little triangle in which she and Sophie played in Sophie's backyard.

Digby Pertwhistle emerged from the house

and stood on the step beside Clementine and Lavender. 'Hello there, you two.'

Clementine looked up and smiled. 'Hello Uncle Digby. Do you think the tent will be finished soon?'

The old man frowned. 'I hope so. There's still a lot to do. At least when the marquee is up, there'll be one less thing for your mother to worry about.'

'What's a marquee?' Clementine asked.

'It's just a fancy name for the tent, Clemmie,' Uncle Digby replied. 'I don't think brides like the idea of having their weddings in a common old canvas tent.'

Clementine felt an excited shiver run through her whole body. She couldn't wait to see the bride in her dress.

'It's a big job,' Clementine declared.

'Yes, it certainly is,' Uncle Digby said. He could recall only one other wedding at the house. It was when a very young and beautiful Violet Appleby had married her first husband. Sadly, the fellow left her and took a lot of her money with him a couple of years later. At the time Uncle Digby was just a young man, and had only started working as the family butler a year before.

'Can Lavender and I help with anything?' Clementine asked.

'Mmm.' Uncle Digby tapped his forefinger against his lip. Most of the remaining jobs involved polishing and cleaning, and letting Clementine loose with a feather duster was not the best idea. Last time she'd helped she had accidentally knocked over one of the family's heirloom vases, chipping the top.

'I've got an idea,' said Uncle Digby. 'Why don't you practise one of your poems and then perhaps you can entertain the guests when they arrive later?'

Clementine nodded. 'I've got that new one you taught me. I could tell it to Mr Bruno and his men. They must get a little bit bored hammering pegs into the ground.'

Uncle Digby smiled at Clementine. 'Just don't get in the way.'

'I won't.' She stood and walked down the steps. 'Come on, Lavender.'

The little pig opened her eyes and scrambled to her feet.

Clementine marched into the garden and climbed onto a bench ready to begin her recital.

One of the older gentlemen working nearby had learned the exact same poem when he was a lad, and soon enough he was saying it along with her.

'You're a clever girl. What's your name?' the man asked when she had finished and taken a bow.

'Clementine,' she replied.

The man grinned at Clemmie. 'Have you got another one for us?'

Clementine loved nothing more than an audience. She knew several poems by heart; her favourite was by a man called Mr Dahl and it was about an anteater. All of the men listened this time. Above the clanking of their hammers, all that could be heard was

Clementine and the odd grunt of approval from Lavender.

Upstairs in the house, Aunt Violet was fiddling with some knick-knacks on her dressing table, when she heard Clementine's voice outside. She wondered what the child could possibly be up to.

The old woman peered through the window. She was horrified to see Clementine nattering at the workmen who'd been stomping about the garden since yesterday afternoon.

Aunt Violet pushed the window up further and poked her head outside. 'Clementine, what are you doing? Those men are here to work, not to listen to your gobbledegook.'

'Oh, hello Aunt Violet,' Clementine called back. 'I'm just practising.'

'You should find somewhere else to do it,' Aunt Violet said. 'Those men don't have time to stand about.'

'But I've no one else to practise with,' said Clementine. She thought of the portraits in the entrance hall. 'Except for Granny and

Grandpa, and they don't laugh as much as these men do.'

'Your grandfather didn't laugh much when he was alive, Clementine. I can't imagine the old trout has changed a jot since he's been dead,' Aunt Violet sneered.

A stout young man looked up at the window. 'It's all right, ma'am. She's not in the way and she's very funny.'

'Clementine, come away from those people at once,' her great-aunt demanded.

'What people?' the young fellow said suspiciously. 'Aren't we good enough to listen to some poetry?'

'I don't know what you mean,' Aunt Violet fumed. 'But I'll be reporting your bad manners to whoever is in charge.'

'That's Mr Bruno.' Clementine pointed at the short fellow in front of her. 'He's the boss.'

Mr Bruno looked up at Aunt Violet's scowling face and then back at Clementine. 'Is she always so lovely?' he asked the girl.

Aunt Violet grumbled something under her breath and then slammed the window so hard that the panes rattled.

'Oh no, she's not lovely at all,' Clementine replied. 'She's Aunt Violet.'

MAGIC

By midday, Mr Bruno and his men had finished their tightening of ropes and hammering of pegs, and in the middle of the back lawn stood an enormous white tent. Clementine thought it looked like a giant wedding cake. Another group of people had arrived and set up lots of round tables, and stacks of chairs were being wheeled into place too.

Clementine and Lavender were having a wonderful time exploring inside, when into the marquee blew the most extraordinary man Clementine had ever seen.

'Oh my, oh my, there's no time, no time, we must get to work. Places everyone, we need to get this show on the road,' he burbled. 'Chop, chop!'

Clementine and Lavender watched from underneath a table. The man wore a bright blue suit, a red bow tie and matching red shoes. A red-and-yellow spotted handkerchief poked out of his blazer pocket. He flapped his hands about as if he were directing traffic at a busy intersection. A stream of people poured into the tent behind him, carrying all manner of things, from huge floral arrangements to rolls of shimmering fabric.

Clemmie's eyes were like dinner plates as she took it all in.

The man clapped his hands together. 'It's not much now, but just you wait and see. Places everyone, let the magic begin.'

Clementine wondered if he was going to put on a show. She scrambled out from under the table and jumped up in front of him.

The man leapt into the air. 'Good gracious, my dear. Where did you come from?'

'Hello,' said Clementine, 'I like your shoes.'

The man peered over the top of his stylish spectacles. 'Oh, thank you. Who do we have here?' His brow furrowed as he caught sight of Lavender, who trotted out and sat beside her mistress.

'I'm Clementine and this is Lavender,' Clemmie replied.

'How darling.' The man surveyed the child in her pretty ensemble and the pig in its matching jumper. He bent down to scratch the top of Lavender's head. She leaned into his fingers and squirmed with delight. 'Aren't you the cutest little piggy in the world? And I just adore your matching outfits.'

'Mrs Mogg made them for us,' Clementine explained. 'Are you a magician?'

A row of lines puckered the man's forehead.

'You said, "Let the magic begin",' Clementine reminded him.

'Yes, yes, I suppose I am a magician of sorts.

Just give me a couple of hours and this tent will go from drab to fab. This wedding is going to be perfect with some magic from Sebastian. That's me, of course. Sebastian Smote at your service.' He rolled his hand and made a bow.

Clementine giggled. 'You're funny.'

'I am here to entertain,' Sebastian replied. 'But dear little girl and dear little piggy, might I suggest that you pop outside to play? When you return, you will not recognize this place, I assure you.'

Clementine would rather have stayed put and watched the magic happen, but she could hear her mother calling her.

Lady Clarissa poked her head inside the entrance. 'I thought you'd be here, Clemmie. Come along and let Mr Smote do his work. It's time for lunch.'

'Goodbye,' Clementine said with a wave. 'I can't wait to see what your magic looks like.'

The man grinned at her, and then hurried away to direct the delivery of an enormous chandelier.

'No, no, no!' he called as there was a loud crash.

'I love weddings,' Clementine enthused as she and her mother walked back to the house, with Lavender a few steps behind. 'Even though I've never been to one before.'

'I just hope it goes smoothly,' said Lady Clarissa. She smiled tensely at her daughter. She'd had at least ten calls that morning from the bride's mother, a pushy woman called Roberta Fox. The last call was about the colour of the soap in the bathrooms. Lady Clarissa had been wondering if she'd made the right decision about having the wedding.

There was also the small challenge of Aunt Violet, who could always be relied upon to upset someone. Lady Clarissa had employed half the village to help with the arrangements and Mr Smote was in charge of making sure it all came together, so with any luck Aunt Violet would stay right out of the way. If it all went well, Lady Clarissa hoped she'd be able to pay for a new roof for Penberthy House without selling the Appleby family jewels after all.

'When will the guests come?' Clemmie asked.

'Everyone's due to arrive this evening,' her mother replied. 'I know you're looking forward to it, Clemmie, but you must remember that *we're* not guests. You can look from a distance but please don't get in the way.'

Clementine nodded. 'I just want to help. And see the bride, of course.'

'Yes, I know you do. It's very important that we get this right. A wedding is one of the biggest events in anyone's life and I want to make sure that the bride and groom have only happy memories of their special day at Penberthy House,' her mother explained.

'Well, you'd better keep Aunt Violet out of the way because she doesn't make anyone very happy,' Clementine said seriously.

'I think she's been trying harder, don't you?' her mother asked, raising her eyebrows.

'Maybe.' Clemmie shrugged. 'I like when she

reads to me. But she was cross about Pharaoh sleeping in my room with Lavender. I told her that she could take Lavender's basket and borrow them for the night and then she said "ick" and pulled a cranky face. But I think she's only pretending. I saw her giving Lavender a scratch the other morning, but when I asked what she was doing she said Lavender was being a nuisance and she was shooing her downstairs.'

Lady Clarissa stifled a grin. 'Never mind, Clemmie. Now, I have lots of jobs to finish this afternoon. Let's get some lunch and then perhaps you can play in your room for a while.'

Lavender grunted as if to agree.

'OK,' Clemmie replied and squeezed her mother's hand.

AUNT VIOLET

Clementine climbed onto a chair opposite her great-aunt at the kitchen table.

'Hello Aunt Violet.'

'Hmph.' The woman didn't look up from the newspaper she was reading.

'Are you excited?' Clementine asked.

Aunt Violet ignored the child completely and kept on reading.

Clementine pinched her forefingers and thumbs together and held them in the air.

'Aren't you just a l-i-i-i-i-ttle bit excited, Aunt Violet?'

Violet Appleby sighed. She folded the newspaper in half and placed it on the table. 'And what exactly should I be excited about? The fact that we're about to be overrun by people I don't care to meet or that there's rain forecast for tomorrow? Mmm?'

Clementine frowned at her great-aunt. 'The wedding. I'm so excited about the wedding and seeing the bride in her beautiful dress. I'm not sure which dress I'll wear tomorrow. I can't decide between my favourite red one and the yellow one Mrs Mogg made me for Christmas last year.'

'Clarissa, the child does realize that she's not *invited* to this ghastly occasion, doesn't she?' Aunt Violet looked at her niece, who was standing at the bench cutting Clementine's cheese sandwich into triangles.

'Of course, Aunt Violet. Clemmie's just excited. We've never had a wedding at the house before and you have to admit, it's always lovely to see a bride on her special day.' Clarissa arranged Clemmie's lunch on a plate and set it down in front of her.

'I can't think of anything worse,' Aunt Violet said with a sneer.

Digby Pertwhistle had been listening to the conversation while he filled the kettle at the sink. He turned and looked at Aunt Violet. 'That's strange, Miss Appleby.'

'Why do you say that?' she asked.

'I thought you must love weddings. Haven't you had four of them?'

'Four!' Clementine looked at her great-aunt. 'Have you been a bride four times?'

'Frankly, that's none of your business,' snapped Aunt Violet. 'And I'll thank you not to bring up the subject ever again, Pertwhistle.'

'You must have been beautiful, Aunt Violet,' Clementine said. 'Especially if you looked like the lady in the painting on the stairs.'

Aunt Violet sniffed. 'Yes, well, I suppose I was rather an attractive young woman.'

'Can you tell me about your dresses?'

Clementine asked. 'Did you wear a white gown?'

'Several, I should think,' Uncle Digby muttered under his breath. Lady Clarissa nudged him.

'Clementine, we are not talking about it. Eat your lunch,' Aunt Violet ordered.

Clementine reluctantly turned her attention to the sandwich on her plate. After a couple of bites she looked up and saw that Aunt Violet was staring at her.

'Would you like some?' Clementine held out a triangle.

'Heavens no. I'll have my own, thank you. That's if anyone could be bothered making me one.'

'What would you like, Aunt Violet?' Clarissa asked.

'Ham and a hint of mustard and some tomato and cheese. Oh, and some of that lovely egg mayonnaise that you make so well.'

'It won't be long,' Clarissa sighed. Her patience for Aunt Violet and her demands was wearing thin, particularly as Clarissa had so many things to do before the guests arrived. 'Aunt Violet?'

'Yes.'

'Digby and I have a lot of jobs to finish this afternoon. Would you mind popping down to Mrs Mogg's and getting a few things for me? And I haven't collected the mail from yesterday, either.'

'I'll come too. We can take Lavender for a walk. She loves going to the village,' Clementine added.

'I don't think so. I'm awfully tired. I was planning to have a rest this afternoon,' Aunt Violet replied bluntly.

'It's all right, Clarissa. I'll go.' Digby patted the young woman on the arm. He hadn't been feeling one hundred per cent himself, but it didn't seem fair for Lady Clarissa to have to run this errand.

'You've got more to do than I have,' Lady Clarissa protested. 'Really, Aunt Violet, we've all got to pitch in.'

'You don't have to use that tone with me, Clarissa,' Aunt Violet barked. She pressed her palm to her forehead. 'I can feel one of my headaches coming on.'

The old woman stood up.

'Where are you going, Aunt Violet?' Clementine asked.

'To my room. Not that it's any of your business.' She walked towards the back stairs. 'You can bring my lunch up when it's ready, Clarissa. And I'd like some tea too. Come, Pharaoh.'

Aunt Violet's sphynx cat had been sleeping in the basket in front of the fire. He arched his back and meowed loudly, before padding over to where Lavender was sitting. He began to lick the side of the little pig's face.

'Urgh. I said come.' Aunt Violet glared at the cat, which ignored her completely. 'Have it your way, then. I think you've been infected by that ghastly pig.'

She stomped upstairs and out of sight.

'Lavender's not ghastly,' Clementine whispered as she disappeared. 'You are!'

Her mother and Uncle Digby remained silent, but they were both thinking exactly the same thing.

AN
OUTING

After lunch, Digby Pertwhistle met Clementine and Lavender at the back door. A chill wind had sprung up and Clementine had put on her favourite pink coat and long snuggly boots with lamb's wool lining.

Uncle Digby grabbed his scarf and coat from the rack beside the door and the trio set off for the village, armed with Lady Clarissa's list.

'Don't forget the mail,' she called after them.

The garden was quiet but inside the marquee

was a hive of activity, with Mr Smote and his assistants in the midst of their decorating. Two large stone lions now guarded the entrance to the tent.

'Look at those!' Clementine gasped. 'How did they get there?'

Uncle Digby pointed to a little tabletop truck with a crane on the back. 'I think that's how.'

'People go to a lot of trouble for weddings, don't they?' Clementine marvelled as she hung back, trying to get another glimpse inside the marquee.

'Come along, Clemmie, we'd best hurry up. I still have some polishing to finish when we get back.' The old man lengthened his stride and Clemmie and Lavender ran to catch up.

Even though she'd almost put Angus's party completely out of her mind, Clementine couldn't help wondering if there might be some mail for her at the store.

By the time they crossed the stream and passed the church to arrive at Mrs Mogg's store, Uncle Digby was completely out of breath.

'Are you all right?' Clementine asked as he sat down heavily on the bench outside.

'Yes, yes, just a bit tired. Must be old age catching up with me.' He smiled reassuringly at Clementine as she tied Lavender's lead to one of the chair legs.

Uncle Digby pushed open the door and the little bell tinkled. Clementine skipped in ahead of him to the toasty warmth of the shop. Today it smelt like hot pies and cinnamon. The old man pulled Lady Clarissa's shopping list from his coat pocket while Clementine went straight to the counter.

Margaret Mogg walked through from the flat that was attached to the back of the building.

'Hello there, Clementine,' she greeted the child warmly. 'And what can I do for you today?'

'Hello Mrs Mogg. Uncle Digby has a list and Mummy asked if I could collect the mail,' Clementine said importantly.

'Of course.' Mrs Mogg turned to the pigeonholes behind the counter. Everyone in the village had their own little cubbyhole for the mail, as there was no postman in Penberthy Floss. 'Well, that's odd.' She peered into the empty space. 'Nothing here at all, Clementine.'

Clemmie frowned. She didn't want to think about Angus's stupid party any more. She wasn't going and that was that.

Mrs Mogg thought it was very unusual. In fact, she couldn't remember a day when there'd been no mail for Lady Clarissa. The woman was always winning competitions and seemed to get an awful lot of bills too.

Mrs Mogg walked back to the counter and looked over at Clementine. 'How are things coming along at the house?'

'Very well, thank you. The marquee is up. That's a fancy name for the tent,' Clementine explained. 'And Mr Smote is decorating it inside and he's even put two giant lions at the entrance to stand guard.'

Mrs Mogg gasped and put her hand to her mouth. 'Lions?'

'Oh, they're not real. They're made of stone. Uncle Digby said that it's probably got something to do with the man who's getting married. He's from another country, and they have lions on their flag,' Clementine explained.

'Ah yes, your mother said that he was Sri Lankan, so that makes sense. I wonder if the bride will wear a white gown or a sari,' Mrs Mogg said.

'What's that?' Clementine asked.

'Saris are beautiful, Clemmie. They're sort of like a wraparound dress but far more complicated and with thousands of sparkles on the fabric,' said Mrs Mogg.

'Can you make one for me?' Clementine asked.

'I don't think so, dear. They're very specialized.'

Clementine was disappointed. She liked the idea of a dress with thousands of sparkles on it.

The doorbell tinkled and Clementine was surprised to see Joshua from school and his mother.

'Good afternoon, Mrs Tribble,' the shopkeeper called.

'Oh hello, Mrs Mogg,' the woman replied. Joshua raced to the counter, his eyes scanning the lolly jars, which contained all manner of treats. He didn't even notice Clementine standing beside him.

His mother reached the counter too. 'I was wondering if you had any cardboard. I have to make his royal highness here a crown for Tuesday.' Mrs Tribble glanced at her son, who was attempting to lift the lid on the container of red frogs.

'It's for Angus's party,' Joshua said. 'I'm going to be a king.'

Clementine felt as if she'd been slugged in the tummy. She decided to go and find Uncle Digby before Joshua noticed her.

'Are you going too, Clementine?' Mrs Mogg asked.

Clemmie quickly shook her head.

'Oh, that's a pity. It must be for the boys,' the old woman said.

'No. It's for girls too. Everyone's going.' Joshua looked at Clementine, and then poked out his tongue at her.

He didn't realize that his mother was watching. She placed her hand firmly on his shoulder. 'Joshua Tribble, last time I looked you were a boy, not a lizard. Apologize at once.'

This time Joshua's mouth stayed closed.

His mother tightened her grip.

'Ow!' Joshua complained. 'You're hurting me.'

The woman leaned down and whispered something into his ear.

'Sorry,' he spat.

'I didn't hear you,' Mrs Tribble said through gritted teeth.

Joshua folded his arms and said with a scowl, 'Sorry, Clementine.'

Clementine said nothing.

Mrs Mogg rubbed her hands together. 'Ahem. Right then. The cardboard is just over in the school supplies.'

'Thank you, Mrs Mogg.' Mrs Tribble grabbed Joshua's hand and headed for the middle of the shop.

'But you said I could have a lolly,' the boy whined.

Clementine couldn't hear exactly what Mrs Tribble said but she thought it sounded like she was going to give him something else.

'Why don't you have a look at some of the lovely new fabrics that came in last week, Clementine?' Mrs Mogg suggested with a smile.

Clementine nodded. Her tummy still didn't feel right, but she walked to the far corner of the shop, where Mrs Mogg kept all of the material, buttons and threads.

Everyone in the village knew about Clemmie's sense of style. Her mother didn't know where it came from, given that the child had arrived in a basket of dinner rolls and been adopted by Lady Clarissa. Clementine and Mrs Mogg shared a love of pretty things. The elderly woman had made Clementine lots of dresses and other bits and pieces over the years. Mr and Mrs Mogg had never had any children, so Clementine was the closest thing they had to a granddaughter and they adored her.

'How are you getting on back there, Digby?'

Mrs Mogg called. 'Is there anything I can help you with?'

Mrs Mogg's shop was always pleasantly heated but today Digby Pertwhistle felt as if he'd walked into a blast furnace. Tiny beads of perspiration formed on his temples and he hastily wiped them away with the back of his hand.

'Yes, thank you, Margaret,' he called back. 'Would you mind locating me some lemon-coloured soap?'

A few minutes later, with Mrs Mogg's help, Uncle Digby had managed to find everything on Clarissa's list and was now standing at the counter packing them into his grocery bag.

'Are you all right, Digby?' Mrs Mogg noticed that his face had turned a rather horrible shade of grey and he seemed to be sweating.

'Yes, it's just a bit warm in here.' He removed his scarf and used it to mop his brow.

'Well, take care of yourself. The last thing Lady Clarissa needs is you getting sick. And tell her I'll be there first thing in the morning to help. Clyde can look after this place for the day.' She was referring to her husband, who preferred watching television to serving in the shop.

Clementine heard Uncle Digby and Mrs Mogg talking and hurried back to them.

'Did you see anything you liked, Clemmie?' the old woman asked.

Clementine shrugged.

'Are you sad about that party?' Mrs Mogg whispered as she leaned forward on the counter.

'A little bit,' Clementine replied.

'Never mind, sweetheart. We can't all go to everything. And no one else is having a wedding at their home this weekend, are they?'

Clementine smiled. 'No, that's true. And I do like the red material with the spots.'

'Ah, that's my girl. I thought you might like that one. Goodbye dear.' Mrs Mogg turned to Uncle Digby. 'And take care of yourself.'

The old man nodded. 'See you tomorrow, Margaret.'

EMERGENCY

lementine, Lavender and Digby Pertwhistle walked up the front driveway just as a black station wagon reversed into one of the parking spaces.

'Looks like some of the guests have arrived early,' Uncle Digby said with a worried look. He had struggled to keep up with Clementine and Lavender on the way home and was feeling far worse than earlier. He was cross with himself for getting sick, and today of all days.

Clementine ran ahead and greeted the

dark-haired man who hopped out of the car. 'Hello. Are you here for the wedding?'

'Yes. My brother's the groom. Are you here for the wedding too?' he asked, wondering if the child was a friend of the bride's family.

'No, I live here with Mummy and Uncle Digby and Lavender.' She motioned towards the pig, which was snuffling about beside her.

'Oh, you're a lucky girl then,' the man replied.

'Except when it rains,' Clementine said.

The man looked at her curiously. 'I don't quite follow.'

Clementine remembered that her mother had told her to stop telling the guests about the leaking roof so she changed the subject. 'It doesn't matter. Are you on your own?'

'No, my wife and children are upstairs getting settled. They'll be thrilled to meet you. And you –' He bent down to give Lavender a scratch. 'I don't think the children have ever seen a pet pig before.'

'She's a teacup,' Clementine said. 'Well, she's a lot bigger than that now.'

'Hello there.' Uncle Digby puffed as he caught up. 'Welcome to Penberthy House. I'm Digby Pertwhistle.'

Just as Uncle Digby said his name, he let out a gasp of air and collapsed to the ground, scattering the groceries all over the place.

'Uncle Digby!' Clementine shouted.

The guest swung into action. 'Run and tell your mother to phone for an ambulance.'

Clementine's face crumpled.

'Don't worry. I'm a doctor.' He smiled at her kindly and then turned his attention to Uncle Digby, who looked as if he was asleep.

Clementine raced up the front steps and into the house. 'Mummy, Mummy,' she called as she ran into the kitchen. Her mother was stirring something on the stove.

Lady Clarissa turned around. 'What is it, Clemmie?'

Clementine's words spilled out in a panicky rush. 'It's Uncle Digby. He's fallen down outside and the man said you need to get an ambulance.' Her mother raced to the telephone and dialled the emergency number. She gave the house's name and address and ran to the front door.

Digby Pertwhistle didn't remember falling over. But now when he tried to lift his head, the whole world seemed to be spinning.

'Mr Pertwhistle you need to lie still,' the man beside him instructed.

'What happened?' Digby asked, holding his hand to his head.

'I'm not sure but we must get you to the hospital for a check-up.'

'No, I can't possibly leave now. There's far too much to do.' Uncle Digby's chest tightened and the words came out as a wheeze.

'Oh, thank heavens,' Lady Clarissa exclaimed as she reached the pair and saw that Uncle Digby was conscious. 'Is he all right, Dr Gunalingam?'

The man was looking at his watch and taking Uncle Digby's pulse. 'Well, he's awake, but I'm not prepared to take any chances. Is the ambulance on its way?'

'Yes, it will be here soon.'

'Is Uncle Digby going to be OK?' Clementine asked.

'Yes, darling, I'm sure he'll be just fine. Can you run upstairs and ask Aunt Violet to come down? Someone needs to go with Uncle Digby to the hospital. And take Lavender inside too,' Lady Clarissa instructed.

In the distance, a siren began to wail.

Clementine called the little pig, who came racing to the front door with her lead bumping along the ground behind her. Clementine ran up the main stairs to the third floor. She barged straight into the Blue Room.

'Aunt Violet,' she said, puffing.

'Haven't you heard of knocking? It's not new, you know.'

Clementine ran back to the door and rapped on it sharply.

'What now?' the old woman grumbled. 'Can't you see I was reading?'

'It's Uncle Digby. He fell down outside and the ambulance is coming,' Clemmie blurted. 'Mummy wants you to go to the hospital with him.'

'Well, why didn't you say so?'

Clementine was confused. She did say so.

Aunt Violet sprang into action. She stood up, smoothed her trousers and shoved her feet into her leopard-print ballet flats. Clementine had never seen her great-aunt move so quickly.

'Come on then, what are you waiting for?' the old woman asked Clementine. 'An invitation?'

Together they rushed down the stairs and out the door. At the front of the house, they saw Uncle Digby lying on the ground, covered by a throw rug that Clarissa had retrieved from the sitting room.

'What's the matter with him?' Aunt Violet demanded. She stared at Digby, whose eyes were wide open and staring back up at her. 'I thought you were dying.'

'Sorry to disappoint you, Miss Appleby.'

'Well, are you sick? Or did you just fall over?' she asked tightly.

Clarissa took her aunt by the arm and guided her away from Uncle Digby and the doctor.

'Dr Gunalingam thinks Uncle Digby might

have something wrong with his heart,' Lady Clarissa whispered. 'I don't want to frighten Clementine but one of us has to go to the hospital with him.'

Aunt Violet pursed her lips. 'Don't look at me. I'm not having Pertwhistle die on my watch.'

'I don't think that will happen but if you're not prepared to go then you'll have to stay here and greet the guests. There are quite a few groups about to arrive,' Clarissa explained.

Aunt Violet was about to tell Lady Clarissa that she couldn't possibly be left in charge when the ambulance roared into the driveway with the lights flashing and siren blaring.

Clementine was sitting beside Uncle Digby holding his hand.

The old man managed a weak smile. 'Don't look so worried, Clemmie. I'll be fine.'

'But I don't want you to go, Uncle Digby.' Tears spilled onto her cheeks.

He squeezed Clemmie's hand. 'Darling girl, it's just a check-up. I'll be back before you've had time to miss me. I can't leave your mother and Aunt Violet with all of the wedding preparations now, can I?'

Clementine shook her head. 'No. Aunt Violet makes Mummy too stressed.'

'Yes, I think you're right about that,' the old man agreed.

The paramedics soon had Uncle Digby on a stretcher and ready to go into the back of the ambulance. Lady Clarissa turned to her aunt. 'Aunt Violet, the bride and her family will be arriving soon. And the groom and his parents too. This lovely man here, who has been so kind and helpful, is Dr Gunalingam, the groom's brother.'

The doctor looked up from where he was monitoring Uncle Digby and nodded at Aunt Violet.

'His wife and their three children are upstairs already. You'll have to arrange some afternoon tea for them, please. Pierre delivered some cakes just a little while ago.' Lady Clarissa ignored Aunt Violet's protests and hugged Clementine,

then climbed into the back of the ambulance. 'Oh, and the room allocations are on the kitchen sideboard. Please make sure that everyone gets the room they're supposed to have.'

The doctor climbed into the back of the ambulance next to Lady Clarissa. 'Please tell my wife where I am,' he called out to Clementine and Aunt Violet.

The driver closed the back doors and ran around to the cabin.

'But, but,' Aunt Violet was aghast. 'Clarissa, you can't leave me in charge. I don't know anything about being hospitable.'

Clementine gave her great-aunt a puzzled look. 'You're not going to the hospital.'

'I said hospitable, Clementine. It means . . . Never mind. I don't know the first thing about how to run this place.'

'Don't worry, Aunt Violet. Lavender and I will help you.' Clementine smiled up at her great-aunt, who seemed to have steam coming out of her ears.

ARRIVALS

After the ambulance left, Clementine and Aunt Violet walked back inside. Her great-aunt began to ascend the stairs.

'Where are you going?' Clementine asked.

'Back to my book,' Violet replied.

'But Mummy said that we need to tell the doctor's wife where her husband is and then make some tea,' she reminded her.

'Godfathers,' Aunt Violet muttered under

her breath and thumped back downstairs. She followed Clementine to the kitchen.

'I can't put the kettle on, but I can help with the cakes,' said Clementine. She noticed a large sponge cake sitting on the sideboard and some of Pierre's chocolate-chip biscuits beside them. She retrieved a little pile of plates from the dresser and put them around the scrubbed pine table.

'They're not taking tea out here,' Aunt Violet protested.

Clementine stopped and thought for a moment. 'I can take everything to the dining room, if you'd like.'

Aunt Violet considered the effort required to move to the other room. 'No, I'm sure the woman and her children will understand, given that we're short-staffed. Set it up out here.'

Clementine carefully placed the cake and the biscuits in the middle of the table.

'You might as well run upstairs and fetch them,' Aunt Violet said reluctantly. She took the kettle off the stovetop and poured the water into the large teapot.

Clementine bounded up the back stairs. She wasn't sure which room the family was in but the Jasmine Suite at the end of the first floor corridor seemed likely. It had two adjoining rooms and Lady Clarissa had recently installed some bunk beds she'd won in a competition. The suite was now perfect for a family staying together.

Clementine knocked on the door. She was greeted by a pretty woman with long dark hair and a very large tummy.

'Hello. My name is Clementine and I live here. Mummy asked me to tell you that your husband has gone to the hospital with Uncle Digby and Mummy, and Aunt Violet and I have made some tea for you and your children,' she explained.

'Oh,' the lady replied. 'I wondered where he'd got to. We heard the siren but couldn't see what was going on. Is everything all right?'

'Uncle Digby fell down. They're just going

to the hospital to check everything's OK,' Clementine explained.

The sound of giggling came from the adjoining room. Clementine craned her neck to see who was making the noise.

'That's the children,' the lady said. 'They've never slept in bunk beds before so they're a little excited. Arya, Alisha, Aksara, come and meet Clementine,' she commanded.

Three children with the most beautiful sparkling brown eyes poked their heads around the doorway and waved.

Clementine giggled as they appeared – one, two, three.

The girls made a dash and hid behind their mother's skirt but the little boy stayed in the doorway.

'They're not really shy.' The woman leaned around and looked at them.

'Would you like to come downstairs?' Clementine asked. 'We have chocolate-chip biscuits and a sponge cake that Uncle Pierre made and he's the best baker in the world.'

At the mention of food the girls skipped out and said hello. The little boy ran over to join them. Clementine led the group down the back stairs and into the kitchen where Aunt Violet was cutting the cake.

'Hello there. I'm Karthika,' the mother introduced herself. 'And this is Arya, who's five, and Alisha, who's three. And Aksara – he's two. This little one is Asha and she'll be here soon.' Karthika patted her belly. 'It's a pleasure to meet you.'

The old woman looked up and glared at the family. 'Yes, I suppose it is.'

'That's Aunt Violet,' Clementine chimed in.

Aunt Violet cut a huge slice of sponge and dumped it roughly onto one of the plates. Clementine wondered why Aunt Violet had to be so cranky. Fortunately, the group was distracted by the front doorbell ringing.

'I'll get it,' Clementine volunteered, but she didn't move.

'Go on, then. I've got my hands full,' Aunt Violet told Clementine. 'And there'd better be nothing wrong with that silly old fool Pertwhistle,' she muttered under her breath. 'I don't know how we'd ever manage without him.'

AUNT VIOLET
MEETS HER MATCH

C lementine opened the front door.
Three people stood in a huddle on
the steps. There was a couple, who
looked older than her mother, but younger than
Uncle Digby, and a very pretty young woman.

'Hello,' said Clementine.

'We're here for the wedding,' said the man
with a look of surprise. He wondered why they
were being met by a child.

'My name is Clementine. Please come in,'
said Clemmie. She was trying to remember

exactly what her mother usually said when she greeted the guests.

The trio walked into the hallway but the lady turned around just as Clemmie was about to close the door. 'Uncle Orville,' she called in a singsong voice. 'Uncle Orville? Where are you?'

'Hector,' the woman said sharply, as she turned and looked at her husband. 'Go and find your uncle. Now!'

Clementine jumped. So did the young woman and Hector. He scurried off outside to locate the missing member of their party.

The woman smiled like a shark at Clementine. 'Where is your mother?'

'Mummy and Uncle Digby have gone to the hospital with the doctor. He's the groom's brother and it was lucky he was here when Uncle Digby fell down. I'm looking after everyone with Aunt Violet,' Clementine explained.

'Oh, I'm sorry to hear that,' said the young woman. 'My name's Harriet Fox.'

'Oh!' Clementine gasped. 'You're the bride. Mummy told me your name.'

The woman beamed. 'Yes, that's right.'

'I can't wait to see your dress. And the tent is going to be so beautiful –' Clementine prattled.

The older woman cut them off. 'Yes, yes, of course she'll be beautiful, she's my daughter. And I should hope we have a marquee and not a tent. Now, if you'll go and fetch your aunt, I'd rather like to get settled in our rooms. We've had a long drive.'

The young woman rolled her eyes at her mother and then smiled secretly at Clementine.

'OK.' Clementine marched off towards the kitchen. Uncle Digby had been right about brides being funny about marquees. Well, bride's mothers.

Meanwhile, Aunt Violet was studying the room allocation list and trying to work out what it all meant. She had a red pen in hand and seemed to be doing some allocating of her own.

'Aunt Violet,' Clementine called. 'The Foxes are here.' Then she giggled. 'I hope the chickens are locked away.'

'What? What chickens? What are you talking about?' Aunt Violet asked the child disdainfully.

Mrs Gunalingam laughed and so did Arya. The woman winked. 'We got it.'

Violet Appleby strode out of the kitchen towards the entrance hall.

'I'd better go too,' said Clementine reluctantly. 'Aunt Violet's not always the most helpful with the guests.'

Mrs Gunalingam nodded. After a few minutes alone with the woman she knew exactly what Clementine was talking about.

Clementine caught up to her great-aunt in the hallway.

'Violet Appleby,' said Aunt Violet as she looked at the mother and daughter. She didn't feel the need for any additional niceties.

'It's lovely to meet you, Miss Appleby.' Harriet Fox extended her hand, which Aunt Violet ignored completely.

'Your rooms are on the second floor. Let me see –' Aunt Violet scanned the list, which was attached to a plastic clipboard. 'Mr and Mrs Fox are in the Peony Suite and Harriet, you're in the Rose Room.'

'What about Uncle Orville? Roberta asked.

Aunt Violet ran her finger down the list. 'He's not here.' She tapped the pen she was holding on the page.

'What do you mean he's not here?' Roberta Fox fumed. 'Of course he's here.' She went to snatch the clipboard from Aunt Violet's hand.

Aunt Violet clutched it to her chest.

'Give me that!' Roberta tugged at the board.

Aunt Violet made a fierce face at her. 'No!'

'Your niece said that she could accommodate the whole family and Uncle Orville is part of the family so I want to see where she has put him.'

Aunt Violet clung to the clipboard.

'Oh look,' Roberta Fox peered over Aunt Violet's shoulder. 'There's Uncle Orville with your father now.'

Aunt Violet turned and just as she did, Roberta Fox tore the clipboard out of her hands.

'Why, you!' Aunt Violet's mouth gaped open.

Roberta scanned the list. 'I think you've been doing some creative rearranging, Miss Appleby. Just wait until your niece gets wind of this.'

'It's my house and I can put people wherever I jolly well want,' Aunt Violet huffed.

Roberta Fox wrinkled her nose like an angry otter. 'Why don't you go and make a fresh pot of tea? This little one can help us find our rooms.'

'I can do that,' Clementine agreed.

Aunt Violet stormed towards the kitchen.

The front door opened and Mr Fox appeared at last with Uncle Orville in tow. The old man wore a smart suit with a waistcoat and a bowler hat. Clementine thought he looked as if his face could do with an iron – there were so many crinkles.

'It says here that Uncle Orville is in the Daffodil Room,' said Mrs Fox.

Clementine gasped. 'But that's my room.' She wondered when her mother had planned to tell her about that.

'All right then, shall we go?' asked Hector Fox. He looked at Clementine, who was suddenly feeling a lot less excited about the wedding party.

Clementine led the group upstairs. First she showed Harriet to the Rose Room, which she seemed to like very much. The Peony Suite was a little further along the corridor. Then she had to take Uncle Orville up to her room. She was surprised when she opened the door to find that most of her things had gone and even her wardrobe was bare. It can't have been a mistake. Her mother had clearly planned to give her room away.

'I hope you like it,' Clementine said grumpily. She looked around for Lavender's basket and even that was missing. 'Stupid wedding,' she said under her breath.

'Thank you, dear,' the old man said. He smiled sweetly at her. 'It's a very nice room.'

'Yes, I know,' she snapped. 'That's because it's mine.'

'No, no, dear, I don't need anything else.

I'll be fine.' The man nodded and put his tiny suitcase on the bed to unpack.

Clementine walked out of the room and down the hallway. She knew she shouldn't be cross about having to give up her room but she wished that her mother had warned her. And why couldn't Aunt Violet have given up her room instead? Clemmie stopped at her mother's bedroom door. She turned the handle and peered inside. Her schoolbag, her doll's house and all her toys were piled in the corner. She opened the wardrobe. Her mother had hung all of Clementine's clothes inside and Lavender's basket was at the bottom. A mattress was made up at the foot of her mother's bed. And in the corner she noticed a large suitcase.

Downstairs, the doorbell rang again. As Clementine scurried downstairs, a terrible thought came to her. She hadn't seen Pharaoh or Lavender for a long time. Her mother would be very unhappy if they'd been locked in one of the guest rooms.

Clementine opened the front door. A

handsome young man was standing on the step. 'Hello,' he said. 'I'm Ryan. The groom.'

'Hello.' Clementine held the clipboard in front of her. She felt very official and important. 'Do you want to check which room you're in?' she asked. 'I can't read much yet. I'm only five.'

The man took the page and had a quick look.

'Here it is. I'm in the Blue Room.'

'The Blue Room?' Clementine said nervously. 'But that's Aunt Violet's room.'

'Sorry? Do you think there's been a mistake?' he asked.

Clementine shook her head. 'No. I'll show you where it is.' She marched upstairs feeling quite pleased. If it was good enough for her to give up her room, then it was good enough for Aunt Violet too.

It wasn't long before the groom's parents arrived, completing the wedding party staying at the house. Clementine helped them to their rooms without any assistance from Aunt Violet, who was still making tea.

Clementine invited everyone to the kitchen – not that Mrs Fox was impressed at all.

Everyone seemed to know each other, which Aunt Violet found a blessed relief. She hated making small talk. Clemmie was pleased to see that Pharaoh and Lavender had emerged from their hiding place and were now playing a vigorous game of chasings with the three children.

'Clementine, why don't you take the children and Lavender for a walk in the garden,' Aunt Violet said testily.

'Oh, I'm not sure about that,' said Karthika anxiously. 'It's getting cold outside.'

'It was *not* a suggestion,' said Aunt Violet.

'Let's go and get your coats, shall we?' Karthika instructed.

The telephone rang and Clemmie ran to pick it up. 'Hello, Penberthy House,' she said, just as her mother had taught her. 'Oh, hello Mummy. Is Uncle Digby all right?'

Her mother could hear the hubbub in the background. 'What's happening there, Clemmie?' she asked.

'Afternoon tea,' the girl replied.

'In the kitchen?' her mother asked.

'Yes, Aunt Violet said that it was a pain to have it in the dining room or the sitting room.'

'Oh, good gracious!' Lady Clarissa fussed. 'These people are paying very good money to stay at the house. I'm sure they didn't expect tea in the kitchen.'

'No, Mrs Fox was very cross,' Clemmie informed her mother quietly, as she didn't want the woman to hear her.

'Did everyone find their rooms?' Clarissa asked.

'Yes,' Clemmie replied.

'Clemmie, I'm sorry about moving you. There was a last-minute change of plans and I didn't have time to tell you or Aunt Violet. Is she very upset?'

'I don't know, but she and Mrs Fox had a fight,' Clemmie explained.

Lady Clarissa groaned. 'I'll be back as soon as I can. Can you ask Aunt Violet to put the legs of lamb in the oven, please? She'll need to peel the potatoes too – they're on the sink. Mrs Mogg will be there in a little while – I called and asked her to help with the dinner.'

'Is Uncle Digby all right?' Clemmie asked her mother again.

'We're not sure,' her mother said truthfully. 'But he's being very well looked after.'

Clementine suddenly felt sick herself. She didn't care about having to share her room with her mother or even Aunt Violet. She just wanted Uncle Digby to be better and back at home where he belonged.

WEDDING EVE

Clementine hung up the telephone and quietly informed Aunt Violet what her mother needed done. Aunt Violet couldn't believe that she was going to have to prepare the evening meal too. This was far too much. She immediately set about clearing the afternoon tea.

'But I haven't finished,' Roberta Fox said in astonishment. She clung to her teacup as Aunt Violet picked up the woman's plate, which still contained a large chunk of cake.

'Perhaps you should eat a little more quickly, Mrs Fox,' Aunt Violet said. 'Some of us have work to do.'

'If you'd served the tea in the sitting room, you wouldn't have this problem now, Miss Appleby.' Roberta tugged the plate from Aunt Violet's grip and set it down with a thud.

Aunt Violet narrowed her eyes. She wasn't about to admit that the woman was probably right.

'Run along, Clementine,' Aunt Violet instructed. 'Take those little ones outside.'

It was the last thing Clementine felt like doing but she decided it was better not to argue with Aunt Violet. She took her coat from the peg by the back door, pulled on her boots and ushered the three children out into the garden. Lavender followed hot on their heels.

'She's lovely,' Alisha said to Clementine as she bent down to give the piggy a scratch.

'Yes, she is,' Clementine agreed. But she couldn't bring herself to smile. She was too worried about Uncle Digby. And lurking in the back of her mind was the unpleasant memory of seeing Joshua at Mrs Mogg's shop. He'd seemed so pleased about Angus's birthday party.

'Are you sad?' Arya asked.

Clementine nodded. 'Uncle Digby never gets sick.' She didn't want to say that she was upset about Angus's stupid party too.

'Don't worry. Our daddy is an expert at broken hearts. I'm sure he can fix your uncle,' Arya told Clementine seriously. She reached out to hold Clementine's hand.

Clementine took it. 'Really?' she asked.

'It's true,' Arya said, smiling now. 'Mummy said that he went to school *for ever* to learn how to do it.'

Clementine felt a little bit better already. 'Would you like to see the garden?'

A chorus of 'yes' went up. It was good to have something to take her mind off Uncle Digby and the hospital, Clementine decided.

'Let's see if Mr Smote has finished his decorations inside the marquee,' Clementine said. 'That's just a fancy name for the tent,' she told the younger two, who nodded their heads up and down.

Aksara ran ahead but jumped back when he saw the lions guarding the entrance. His eyes were huge.

'It's all right,' Clementine reassured the little boy. 'They're not real.' She pulled back the heavy fabric that had been hung across the doorway. He tiptoed past the lions.

Clementine gasped as she took in the decorations. 'Mr Smote *is* a magician.'

The ceiling was draped with the most beautiful shimmering silver fabric and a giant crystal chandelier hung from the centre. The chairs looked like presents, wrapped up with bows on their backs, and the tables were laid with shiny silverware and white plates with silver trim.

Clementine spied the magician himself on the far side of the marquee, and walked towards him. 'Hello Mr Smote.'

'Hello there, Clementine. What do you

think?' He held his arms out with a flourish.

'It's beautiful,' Clemmie sighed.

'And the flowers aren't even here yet.' He rubbed his hands together. 'Just wait until you see it tomorrow morning.'

'Mummy says I can only poke my head in. I'm not going to the wedding, but my friends are.' She motioned at the children who were standing beside her. 'It's their uncle who's getting married.'

'Well, I do hope that you enjoy yourselves,' Mr Smote said. 'And what do you think of my lions?'

Aksara looked up at him with wide eyes. 'Big.'

The girls giggled.

'Yes, they are, aren't they? I've heard that the groom loves them,' said Mr Smote.

Arya nodded. 'Our daddy's his brother and he does too.'

'Well, you'd better be running along. I have to get home to paint a castle,' said Mr Smote.

'A castle?' Clementine gasped. Penberthy

House was big enough. She couldn't imagine what it would be like to live in a castle.

'How do you paint a castle?' Arya asked.

Mr Smote looked at the children's stunned faces. 'Oh no, I'm not painting a real castle. My godson is having a birthday party next week and I offered to create a miniature castle for the party.'

Clementine couldn't believe her ears. She wondered if Mr Smote was *Angus's* godfather. If he was in charge of the party then it would be incredible for sure. She wished even harder now that she could go.

'All right, I'm about to lock up for the night,' Mr Smote said as he walked towards the entrance.

Clementine was curious about how he could do that. Tents didn't have proper doors, after all.

'You don't need to lock up,' Arya said.

'Why not?' Mr Smote asked

'Because there are lions on guard,' she said with a smile.

Mr Smote laughed. 'Yes, you're right about that.'

'And a pig too,' Clementine added. Lavender was sitting right in the middle of the two stone beasts.

'She's a guard pig,' Alisha giggled. Lavender grunted as if to agree.

The children headed back inside just before dark. Clementine had decided the best thing she could do was forget all about Angus and his party and concentrate on the wedding and playing with her three new friends.

Mrs Gunalingam met them at the back door and guided her children straight upstairs to their baths.

Inside, Margaret Mogg was stirring the gravy on the stove. Clementine stood on tiptoe to watch. 'I'm glad you're here, Mrs Mogg.'

'We couldn't let the guests starve, could we?' said Mrs Mogg. She left the wooden spoon in the saucepan and opened the oven to check on the lamb.

Clementine's nostrils twitched. 'It smells delicious. Is Mummy home yet?'

'She telephoned a little while ago. Aunt Violet is driving over to pick her and the doctor up,' Mrs Mogg explained.

'That's a relief,' said Clementine.

The sound of the front door opening distracted the pair and Clementine ran off into the hallway.

'Mummy!' Clementine launched herself at her mother's waist. From out of nowhere, tears sprang from her eyes and she began to cry in big shuddery sobs.

'Oh Clemmie, sweetheart, what is it?' Her mother knelt down and Clementine clung to her like a periwinkle in a rock pool.

'I – don't – know,' she gulped.

'Clemmie, Uncle Digby will be fine. Please don't worry. He wouldn't want to see you like this.'

Lady Clarissa brushed a rogue strand of hair

from Clementine's wet face. 'I know it's been a difficult day, what with all the excitement of the wedding and then the worry about Uncle Digby. But I'm sure that tomorrow will be much brighter.'

Clementine didn't tell her that she'd been upset about seeing Joshua and hearing Mr Smote talk about a party too, or that she was mad about having to give up her room, or that Aunt Violet had been even crosser than usual. She didn't want to sound like a crybaby.

'Come along, Clemmie. Let's go and wash your face and then we can get ready for dinner. Mrs Mogg has been busy – something smells delicious.'

Lady Clarissa stood up. Clementine grabbed her hand and the two of them walked to the downstairs bathroom where Clementine splashed some water on her face and dried her eyes.

'Where's Aunt Violet?' Clementine asked between sniffs.

'She went straight upstairs to move her

things into Uncle Digby's room for the night. I had to tell her in the car that I'd given her room away too and she'd be bunking in with us. But now, of course, with Uncle Digby away, she's decided to take his room. She wasn't nearly as cross as I expected but I think that was because Dr Gunalingam was in the car too. No doubt I'll hear about it later when everyone's gone home.'

Clementine nodded. Her mother was right about that.

No one noticed the little pile of mail on the hall table. Just as Aunt Violet had been about to leave to pick up Lady Clarissa and the doctor, Father Bob had turned up on the doorstep clutching a bundle of letters that had been among his mail. He'd been very surprised to find them, as Mrs Mogg never made mistakes with the post. Then again, she had left Mr Mogg in charge on Thursday afternoon when she'd been helping at Penberthy House and Clyde wasn't known for his attention to detail.

NIGHT
TERRORS

Lady Clarissa glanced at the kitchen clock. It was already past midnight and she had just finished the washing up and sent Margaret Mogg on her way. Fortunately, dinner had gone well and the guests seemed to be enjoying themselves. She thought that the bride and groom seemed very well suited, although Roberta Fox had certainly not been any less demanding in person. Clarissa had been glad when Aunt Violet skulked off to bed early complaining of another imaginary ailment. Her aunt had done enough damage that day and Clarissa thought she couldn't possibly upset anyone from her bed.

In the eerie quiet, Lady Clarissa wondered if Uncle Digby was all right. She missed him terribly; over the years she'd come to rely on him as much as she would have her own father. A tear spilled onto her cheek and she brushed it away. She couldn't bear the thought of anything happening to him. She shook the notion from her head. Of course he'd be fine – there wasn't any other option.

Meanwhile upstairs, Aunt Violet awoke wishing she hadn't had that last cup of tea before bed. She peered into the darkness. After a few moments she remembered that she had been banished to Pertwhistle's bedroom, which at least had a bathroom attached. In fact, it wasn't a bad room at all. Perhaps she'd swap. She tottered off to the toilet, not bothering to put on the light.

Further down the hallway, Orville Fox felt the same urge. He put on his dressing-gown and slippers and headed along the corridor to the bathroom. A few minutes later, he shuffled back to his room and opened the door, stubbing his toe and wondering who had put the wooden trunk near the bed in the time he'd been out.

Orville sat down, took off his slippers and eased out of his gown. He adjusted the pillows and rolled onto his side and within just a few seconds he was fast asleep.

Lady Clarissa finished drying the last saucepan. From somewhere high in the house, a bloodcurdling scream shook the windows. She leapt into the air, threw the saucepan onto the bench with a clatter and ran up the back stairs two at a time.

Clementine woke with a start. She sprang out of bed and ran along the corridor towards Uncle Digby's room. There was an awful noise coming from inside. When she opened the door and flicked on the light, her eyes almost popped out of her head.

'Aunt Violet, what's going on?' she gasped.

Lady Clarissa ran into the room behind her.

Violet Appleby was standing beside the bed, her face as white as a sheet and her hair standing on end as if she'd poked her finger into a power point. Her breathing was shallow and she looked as if she was trying to speak.

'Mummy, there's a man in Aunt Violet's bed!' Clementine exclaimed.

'Get him out of here!' Aunt Violet shrieked, prodding the intruder's side with her forefinger. 'Get him out of here NOW!'

But Orville Fox was sound asleep. Clearly the man could have slept through a cyclone, because he'd just met Hurricane Violet.

MIXED UP

Clementine rubbed her eyes. For a moment she had forgotten where she was. She took a few seconds to remember that she was on a mattress at the foot of her mother's four-poster bed.

She could hear the pitter-patter of raindrops against the window.

'Mummy,' Clementine called. But there was no reply. She sat up and saw that her mother's bed was already made.

Clementine threw back the covers and

shivered. Lavender and Pharaoh were curled up together in Lavender's basket near the radiator.

She grabbed her dressing-gown, stuffed her feet into her woolly slippers and headed out along the corridor to the back stairs. As she passed by her own bedroom, the door opened and she was met by Uncle Orville.

He must have stayed put after his earlier adventure. Half the house had come running after Aunt Violet's scream. In the end, Mr Fox and Dr Gunalingam had carried Uncle Orville back to Clementine's room, much to the relief of Aunt Violet. She said that she was going to barricade the door.

The man squinted at Clemmie. 'Hello dear.'

'Good morning, Mr Fox,' she said. 'Did you have a good sleep?'

'Yesh, yesh, but I had a terrible dream about a wild woman who was shcreaming like a witch . . .'

Clementine wondered why he was talking strangely.

'Are you joining ush for the wedding today?' he asked.

Clementine couldn't believe that she'd almost forgotten about it. Of course, that's why Mr Fox was dressed up. He might have been old and a little off kilter, but he was a very snappy dresser.

'I like your suit,' Clementine said, admiring the pinstripes and the lovely silk handkerchief that was poking out of his pocket. 'But you might want to change your shoes.'

Mr Fox looked down at his slippered feet.

'Oopsh.' He turned and walked back into the room. 'I wash a tailor you know.'

'Really?' Clementine was impressed. 'Mrs Mogg makes all my clothes. I think she's very clever. She can make just about anything . . . Although, I don't know if she could make a suit.' She followed him inside the room.

Clementine glanced at her bedside table and noticed what she first thought was a glass of water. Then she looked more closely.

'Mr Fox, I think you've forgotten something else too,' she said, pointing.

'Oh, thank heavensh.' Mr Fox shuffled over and reached into the glass. He popped his teeth into his mouth and gave Clementine a big smile.

Other children her age might have been frightened, but Clementine had seen plenty of false teeth at the house before. In fact, she even had a couple of sets that guests had left behind. She sometimes made up plays with the talking teeth, much to her mother's and Uncle Digby's horror.

'You look very nice, Mr Fox,' said Clementine, grinning back at him. 'Even better with your teeth.'

Clementine said goodbye and raced down the back stairs to find her mother and Mrs Mogg busily preparing breakfast. Violet Appleby was dressed and sitting at the table sipping a cup of tea.

'Oh, hello, sleepyhead.' Her mother glanced at the clock on the wall. It was half past nine.

'Half the day's gone, Clementine,' her great-aunt commented. 'Why don't you run along and get dressed. I presume you still want to see that wedding?'

'Yes, of course,' said Clementine.

The smell of bacon filled the room as Mrs Mogg opened the oven and retrieved a plate piled with crispy rashers. She trotted off to the dining room.

'Would you like something to eat first, Clemmie?' her mother asked.

The child nodded. Her stomach was making all sorts of funny gurgles.

'What about an egg and some bacon on toast?' her mother suggested.

'Yes, please.'

Lady Clarissa turned to her aunt. 'Aunt Violet, would you like to see Uncle Digby this morning? Then I'll go later tonight.'

Clementine looked up expectantly. She'd hoped Uncle Digby would be home today.

'No,' Aunt Violet said tersely. 'I'm far too tired. Some of us didn't have a good night at all.'

'But that's not Mummy's fault,' said Clementine.

'Of course it is,' Aunt Violet snapped. 'If she'd bothered to have locks installed on the bedroom doors, I'd never have been confronted by that ghastly man – who, by the way, was missing his teeth!'

Lady Clarissa changed the subject. 'Well, Aunt Violet, do you think you could manage to give Mrs Mogg a hand this morning with some tidying up? The caterers will be here soon – thankfully everything is pre-prepared and they just have to use the ovens to heat things up.'

'I'm exhausted, Clarissa,' Violet snapped. 'And you've employed half the village to help. Why do I have to get involved?'

Lady Clarissa stood firm. 'Aunt Violet, with Uncle Digby in hospital we are still short-staffed.'

'Well, it's just like him to bunk off when we're busy,' Aunt Violet complained.

Clementine had been getting crosser by the second. 'It's your fault Uncle Digby's not here!'

'I beg your pardon, young lady?' Aunt Violet turned sharply to look at the girl.

'If you hadn't made Uncle Digby go to the shop with me yesterday afternoon he'd still be all right. You made him sick!' Clementine pushed the plate of bacon and eggs so hard that the bacon scattered all over the table.

'How dare you?' Aunt Violet's lip trembled. 'I did no such thing, Clementine.' She stood up and strode towards the back stairs.

Clementine began to cry. She'd never felt so mixed up inside. One minute she was excited and the next minute she was worried about Uncle Digby or sad that she hadn't been invited to Angus's party. Clementine didn't like it at all.

Lady Clarissa rushed over and wrapped her arms around Clementine, giving her a big hug.

'I'm sorry, Mummy,' the girl sniffed. 'I didn't mean to upset Aunt Violet.'

'It's all right, darling. I know we all want Uncle Digby home as soon as possible. But really, it's not Aunt Violet's fault that Uncle Digby is sick.' Lady Clarissa kissed her daughter's cheek.

'Why don't you finish your breakfast, then run along upstairs and get dressed. I'm sure that Mrs Mogg would love to see you in one of her pretty dresses. And then you can pop out into the garden with Lavender and watch everything from there.'

Mrs Mogg smiled at Clementine, who sniffled once more and then nodded back.

AUNT VIOLET
TO THE RESCUE

lementine did exactly as her mother suggested. She put on one of her favourite dresses, a lovely red one with a matching coat. She added her shiny red boots and finished off the ensemble with a bow in her hair and a scarf around her neck.

Clementine was on her way downstairs when a shriek filled the house. She ran down to the second floor, and was greeted on the landing by the bride's mother. Mrs Fox was wrapped in a towel and dripping water all over the floor.

'Tell your mother there's no hot water,' Roberta Fox shouted at Clementine. 'How am I supposed to get ready for the biggest day in my life when I can't even have a hot shower?'

Her husband Hector emerged, already dressed, from the bedroom.

'That's funny, dear. I thought it was the biggest day in our daughter's life,' he chided.

'You know what I mean, Hector. Just go and find someone to fix it. NOW!' she screeched.

Orville Fox was on his way downstairs when he ran into the group.

The old man winked at his niece-in-law. 'I'm afraid you might have to put on more than that for the wedding.'

His nephew chortled loudly. 'I was thinking just the same thing myself, Uncle Orville.'

'Oh, stop being ridiculous, the pair of you!' Roberta glared at her husband and his uncle, who scurried away downstairs.

Clementine was just about to suggest that

Mrs Fox could use the bathroom upstairs instead, when Aunt Violet appeared.

She pushed past the woman and straight into the bathroom. Clementine dashed after her. She was surprised to see Aunt Violet giving the taps some rather violent attention, and then banging on the old boiler in the corner.

'That's done it,' Aunt Violet announced as she ran the taps. Steam began to pour from the room.

Clementine stared at her great-aunt in amazement. 'You fixed it!'

'Of course I did.' The old woman strode back into the hallway and Clementine followed.

Roberta Fox barged into the bathroom and slammed the door.

'Don't bother thanking me.' Aunt Violet pursed her lips and hurried away down the corridor with Clementine close behind.

'But how did you do that? Mummy says that Uncle Digby is the only one who can ever fix the hot water in there,' Clementine said.

'I lived here for a long time too, Clementine,'

Aunt Violet replied. 'And that heater has been the same ever since I can remember.'

'I thought Mrs Fox was going to burst, she was so cross.' Clementine smothered a giggle as she remembered the woman's expression.

'Well, we wouldn't want that now, would we?' Violet kept her eyes straight ahead and walked towards the main stairs.

'Aunt Violet?' Clementine called.

'What is it this time?' The old woman turned and stared at Clementine. She couldn't help thinking that the child looked rather sweet in her red ensemble.

'I'm sorry about what I said before. Uncle Digby isn't sick because of you.'

The woman coughed sharply and turned away. 'Don't be so sure of that,' she mumbled, but Clementine didn't hear her.

'Do you want to go for a walk outside?' Clementine asked.

'I'll come with you in a little while,' Aunt Violet replied. 'Mrs Mogg needs some help first.'

Clementine could hardly believe her ears. She wondered if something had happened to Aunt Violet. Clemmie glanced up at the portraits on the wall. Maybe her grandpa had had a word.

THE BEST
DAY EVER

Clementine ran downstairs and threw open the front door. There were cars all over the driveway and Mr Smote was barking orders as tall floral arrangements were carried through the garden towards the marquee.

'Hello Mr Smote,' Clementine shouted.

'Good morning, Clementine,' he called back.

She thought his clothes looked even smarter than the day before. 'That's a lovely tie.'

'Why, thank you, Miss Appleby,' he said and dipped into a bow.

The clock in the hall chimed and Clementine counted off the strikes. She wondered where Harriet Fox was – it couldn't be too much longer until the wedding. Her mother had said that it would start at midday and the clock had just chimed eleven times.

A white van pulled up and two men jumped out and began unloading a pile of enormous presents wrapped in silver paper with white bows.

'Oh!' Clementine gasped. 'They're so pretty.'

And that's when the idea came to her. She should find Uncle Digby a present to cheer him up. Not just any old present; this one had to be perfect, so that he'd know how much she wanted him to get well and come home.

Clementine wondered what she could get him. She didn't have very much money in her piggy bank. And the only shop close by was Mrs Mogg's, and she didn't really sell a lot of things Clemmie thought Uncle Digby would like.

Maybe she could ask her mother to take her to the village later on, once the wedding was underway. Clementine closed the door and turned around. At the top of the stairs she saw the most extraordinary sight.

'You look like a princess,' Clementine gasped, as she took in Harriet Fox's beautiful gown. It was white and covered with silver sparkles. Her long blonde hair was pulled back into a perfect bun and she was wearing a shiny tiara.

Harriet beamed. 'Thank you, Clementine. I feel like a princess today. Have you seen the children?'

Clementine shook her head.

'They're in the wedding too. Arya and Alisha are my flower girls and Aksara is the pageboy,' Harriet explained.

Clementine couldn't wait to see them all. A moment later, Mrs Gunalingam appeared on the landing behind Harriet with the three children in tow. She was wearing a beautiful purple and red wraparound dress with thousands of tiny sparkles all over it. Right behind her, the two little girls wore the prettiest white dresses, which were tied at the waist with large purple bows. Their tiny brother wore a black suit with a sparkly purple bow tie.

'You all look beautiful,' Clementine gasped. She remembered her conversation with Mrs Mogg at the shop. 'Is that a sari?'

'That's right, Clementine.' The woman spun around to show off the whole garment.

'It's so pretty,' Clemmie said.

A man carrying a huge camera skirted the group at the top of the stairs and walked halfway down. He pulled out the tripod legs and set up to take some photographs.

'We'll take some more shots inside the house before we head out into the garden,' he instructed.

He arranged the children on the stairs in front of the bride. Clementine watched, spellbound. When they finally moved into the front sitting room for some seated pictures, Mrs Gunalingam whispered something to the photographer.

'Yes, of course, ask her to join us.'

'Clementine, would you like to have a picture with Harriet and the children?' Mrs Gunalingam asked.

Clementine clapped her hands together. 'Yes, please.'

The man showed the group to their positions and then snapped away. Clementine beamed for the camera.

Mr and Mrs Fox arrived downstairs with Uncle Orville. Clementine decided that she would go and find her mother, Aunt Violet and Mrs Mogg, and let them know that the wedding was about to start. They could watch from the garden.

Lavender was snuffling about Clemmie's feet as she entered the kitchen. She clipped the little pig's red lead onto her collar. She thought she'd better not risk upsetting the guests by allowing Lavender to wander around on her own.

Outside, a large group of people had gathered in the walled garden for the ceremony. Clementine admired all of the gorgeous outfits;

there were women wearing sparkly saris like Mrs Gunalingam's and others dressed in pretty gowns. The men looked handsome too. And Mr Smote was smiling as he watched on from the side. The rain had cleared and the sun was shining.

Clementine stood between her mother and great-aunt as Harriet Fox and her father walked down the makeshift aisle behind the three dark-haired children. A string quartet played and Clementine thought it was the most beautiful music she'd ever heard.

Everyone oohed and aahed as Aksara tried to scatter rose petals from a little basket. He soon grew tired of his job and tipped the basket upside down, dumping a pile of petals onto Uncle Orville's foot. The guests roared with laughter.

During the ceremony, the bride and groom said a lot of words before exchanging rings. Then they kissed. Clementine closed her eyes. Kissing was yucky.

Afterwards, the guests moved into the marquee while the bride and groom posed for photographs with their family. Clementine loved watching the children climb up onto the lions outside the tent for a special picture.

'Well, that's that then.' Mrs Mogg smiled at Clementine. 'What did you think?'

'It was beautiful. I can't wait to be a bride. But I don't want to have to kiss a boy.' Clementine screwed up her face at the thought.

Aunt Violet raised her eyebrows. 'I think that's a long way off, young lady.'

'I should think so.' Her mother laughed and squeezed her hand.

'I don't know about you lot, but there's a warm fire and a cup of tea inside,' Mrs Mogg said. She turned to go.

'That is an excellent plan,' Aunt Violet nodded.

Clementine shivered. 'Won't they be cold out here in the tent?'

'Oh no, I had a quick peek earlier. Would you believe they have heaters in there? At least if it rains it will be drier than inside the house,' Mrs Mogg declared.

'Perhaps you should leave the tent up, Clarissa, and we can all move in there,' Aunt Violet suggested, raising her eyebrows playfully.

'You might be right about that, Aunt Violet. We'll have to move out when I can afford for the roof to be done.'

Clementine looked at her mother. 'We won't really have to live in a tent, will we, Mummy?'

'No darling, I'm sure that we can find somewhere else just for a little while,' her mother replied.

'Perhaps you should all head off on a holiday,' Mrs Mogg suggested.

'Yes please.' Clemmie clapped her hands together.

'Maybe.' Lady Clarissa slipped her hand into Clementine's and together the group headed back inside to the snuggly warmth of the kitchen.

Mrs Mogg filled the kettle and Aunt Violet went to the sideboard to find some cups and saucers. Clementine wondered if there was something wrong with her – she was being so helpful.

Her mother went to the pantry to fetch the teacake Pierre had delivered that morning along with the giant layered wedding cake.

Lavender was lying on her back and enjoying a belly scratch from Clementine.

'Oh, that reminds me, was there any mail yesterday?' Lady Clarissa asked as she set the cake on the table.

Margaret Mogg turned from where she was pouring the tea. 'No. It was very strange indeed.'

Violet Appleby coughed, then scurried from the room. When she returned, she placed a bundle of letters on the table. 'Father Bob brought these over yesterday afternoon as I was leaving to pick you up, Clarissa. He said that it was in among his. I completely forgot about it too. It's probably just bills, anyway, although you do seem to have a knack with those competitions.'

Margaret Mogg sighed deeply. 'I can't leave

that husband of mine in charge for more than a minute. I am so sorry, Clarissa. I hope there wasn't anything important.'

Clementine washed her hands and sat up at the table beside her great-aunt. She looked at the letters, trying not to get her hopes up again.

Lady Clarissa flicked through the pile. 'Bill, bill, bill. Oh!' She drew in a sharp breath and handed Clementine an envelope. 'This one's for you.' 'For me? What is it?' she asked, her eyes wide.

Clementine tore open the envelope and unfolded the card inside. There was a picture of a king and her name was beside it in large scribbly writing.

'What does it say?' she said excitedly, and showed the card to Aunt Violet.

'Wait a minute, I have to get my glasses.' The old woman picked them up from the table. 'It says, "You are invited, Clementine Rose!"'

'Yippee!' Clementine's arms shot into the air. 'He didn't leave me out on purpose.'

Her great-aunt scowled at the interruption. 'Do you want to hear the rest?'

'Yes, please.' Clementine clapped her hands together.

Aunt Violet read the details, including what time and where the party would take place.

Clementine's mouth fell open. 'Oh!'

'What's the matter now?' her great-aunt asked. 'I thought you wanted to go to the party – even though you pretended that you didn't.'

'I don't have a present. Angus said that we all had to get him something good or he'd feed us to the dragon that lives at the bottom of his garden,' Clementine said seriously.

'For heaven's sake. I wouldn't want to go to his party if he said that to me,' Aunt Violet declared. 'And you do know that there are no dragons living at the bottom of his garden, don't you? The boy has an overactive imagination.'

Clementine was not so sure. Angus could be very convincing when he wanted to be.

'Will you take me to the village later?' Clementine asked her mother. 'I have to find the perfect present for Uncle Digby too.'

Mrs Mogg poured three cups of strong black tea.

'Oh darling, I don't think I have time today. But perhaps . . .' Lady Clarissa glanced at Aunt Violet.

Clemmie followed her gaze. 'Aunt Violet, will you take me? Please?' Clementine looked up at the older woman, her blue eyes sparkling.

'I don't know, Clementine. I have some things to do . . .' Aunt Violet sipped her tea.

'Pretty please?'

Aunt Violet stared at the girl's pleading expression. 'Oh, all right,' she relented.

Lady Clarissa and Mrs Mogg exchanged smiles.

Clementine couldn't believe it. She'd just been to her first wedding and next week she was going to a birthday party with all her friends. *And* Aunt Violet had agreed to help her find the perfect presents for Angus and Uncle Digby.

THE SEARCH

Clementine and Aunt Violet put on their coats and headed out into the afternoon sunshine. When Clemmie had asked Lavender if she wanted to go for a walk, the little pig had rolled over and kept her eyes firmly closed. Pharaoh was asleep too. He slept a lot.

Loud music filled the garden and Clementine wanted to stop and have another peek at what was happening. She and Aunt Violet poked their heads inside the marquee and laughed when they saw Uncle Orville on the dance floor copying the moves of some beautiful young women in saris.

'Silly old fool,' Aunt Violet huffed.

Clementine giggled.

Mr Smote was standing near the entrance and overseeing the celebration when he noticed Aunt Violet and Clementine. He shuffled over beside them. 'It's all going beautifully,' he said happily. 'I think we could definitely recommend Penberthy House for more weddings.'

'That's wonderful,' Clementine replied. 'Mummy will be so pleased, won't she, Aunt Violet?'

Aunt Violet looked as if she had trodden in something smelly. 'I suppose so.'

The pair said goodbye to Mr Smote and continued through the field at the back of the garden, across the stone bridge and past the church to the Moggs' shop.

'Do you know what you're looking for, Clementine?' her great-aunt asked as they made their way inside.

Clementine shook her head. She hadn't a clue, but thought she might know when she saw it.

Unfortunately, Mrs Mogg's range of toys was rather small and hardly any were suitable for Angus. Clementine searched and searched but nothing was right.

When it came to finding something for Uncle Digby, she considered several options. He liked aftershave, but she knew that he only wore a certain kind. A new pen could be nice, but there were only plain ones. At last Clementine remembered that he liked to play cards, but she couldn't find any. Mr Mogg said that Father Bob had bought the last set earlier in the day.

This was turning out to be much harder than Clemmie had thought.

'Why don't you just make Pertwhistle a card and be done with it?' Aunt Violet suggested.

Clementine supposed she could do that, but it still didn't solve the problem of finding something for Angus.

'Your mother might be able to get something tomorrow over at Highton Mill,' her great-aunt said. 'Or, even better, doesn't she have a present cupboard at home?'

Clementine nodded. Of course she did. Why hadn't she thought of that earlier? Her mother had won so many things over the years that she had a whole cupboard full of bits and pieces. Surely Clemmie could find something in there.

Clementine and Aunt Violet said goodbye to Mr Mogg, who seemed very happy to see them go. It probably had something to do with the sound of football on the television out the back. On the way home, Clementine stopped several times to pick up coloured leaves, which she thought she could use to decorate her card for Uncle Digby.

Clementine was leaning down beside the stone wall when she jumped back in surprise. There was something wedged in the wall.

'Aunt Violet,' she called. 'Come and look at this.'

Her great-aunt sniffed and sauntered over.

'What's that?' Clementine pointed at the wall.

Aunt Violet peered into the space. 'My goodness. I haven't seen one of those in years. Not since I was a girl.' She reached in and carefully pulled out the strange object.

Clementine looked at her wide-eyed. 'Does it bite?' she asked.

Aunt Violet laughed. 'No, Clementine, of course not.'

Clementine had never seen anything so beautiful. 'It's lovely.'

'Yes, and very rare too, I think. I seem to recall Pertwhistle having a collection of these when he first came to work at the house.'

'Really?' Clementine asked.

'Yes. He kept them on the windowsill in the kitchen.'

'Do you think he'd like it?' Clementine asked.

'I suspect it would be perfect,' Aunt Violet said with a nod. 'It's very fragile, Clementine. Why don't we take it home and wrap it up safely?'

Clementine agreed. Now she just had to find the perfect present for Angus too.

PEACE AND QUIET

L ady Clarissa was thrilled with Clementine and Aunt Violet's find. She located a box and helped Clementine wrap it carefully. A quick search through the present cupboard revealed many treasures a little boy would love. Clementine found something she thought would be just right and her mother helped her wrap it as well.

'Why don't you make the cards for Uncle Digby and Angus?' her mother suggested. 'Then we can tape them to the boxes and make sure they don't get mixed up.'

Lady Clarissa frowned. She probably should have found some different wrapping paper for each present but that was the one thing she'd been running low on.

Early in the evening, Mrs Fox appeared at the kitchen door. Aunt Violet and Clementine were at the table reading together and Lady Clarissa was busy getting the household's dinner ready. She was wondering how late the festivities in the garden would continue.

'Ahem,' said Mrs Fox.

Lady Clarissa stopped chopping the carrots and turned around. 'Oh, hello. Please come in.'

'I'd just like to give you this.' Mrs Fox held out an envelope.

'Is the wedding over?' Clarissa asked.

'Yes, Harriet and Ryan left a few minutes ago and we're about to pack up and head home too,' Mrs Fox said.

'I hope it all went well?' Lady Clarissa felt a little scared to ask. Mrs Fox hadn't been the easiest of house guests.

Mrs Fox beamed. 'Marvellous. Hector and

I couldn't have been more thrilled. The food was stunning, the setting was beautiful and Mr Smote – well, the man's a magician.'

Clementine smiled to herself. She knew that already.

'I'm so glad you've had a good day,' Lady Clarissa said with a relieved smile. 'And I'm sorry about not being here when you arrived.'

'Don't worry yourself about that,' Mrs Fox tutted. 'I just hope that Mr Pertwhistle is better soon. Heaven knows we *all* have our challenges with the elderly.'

Aunt Violet frowned.

'Uncle Orville, of course,' Mrs Fox said quickly.

'Oh, of course,' said Aunt Violet, nodding.

Lady Clarissa took the envelope and put it on the sideboard. She rather hoped its contents might cover the new roof. 'I'll see you off then.' She led Mrs Fox to the front hall.

Clementine followed, and bumped into Dr Gunalingam at the bottom of the stairs. He was bringing down the last of his family's bags.

'Goodbye, Clementine,' the man said. 'It was lovely to meet you.'

'Have the children gone already?' Clementine asked. She was hoping to say goodbye to Arya, Alisha and Aksara. 'They're all sound asleep in the car, I'm afraid. And Clemmie –' Dr Gunalingam looked at her seriously – 'I'm sure that Mr Pertwhistle will be fine.'

Clementine beamed. 'Thank you. Please say goodbye to Mrs Gunalingam and the children from me.'

Clementine joined her mother at the front door. As the Gunalingams' and the Foxes' cars drove away, she turned to her mother.

'Can you help me find my princess dress?' she asked.

'Of course, darling. And I have a surprise for you too.'

Clementine looked up at her mother. 'A surprise?'

'Yes, the hospital called a little while ago. Uncle Digby should be home on Tuesday.'

Clementine beamed.

PERFECT

Clementine couldn't wait to tell her friends that she was going to Angus's party too. Her mother had telephoned Mrs Archibald on Sunday afternoon to apologize for their very late RSVP and explained the mix-up with the mail. Mrs Archibald told Clarissa that Angus had been sad that Clementine wasn't coming to his party, but he'd be very happy now.

Clementine wondered if that was true or if Mrs Archibald had just said it to be kind. But when she got to school, Angus ran straight up to her.

'I'm glad you're coming to my party,' he said, grinning.

'Thank you, Angus,' Clementine replied.

'Yeah, 'cos now my dragon will have something tasty to eat.'

Poppy rolled her eyes at him. 'You don't even have a dragon.'

'Yes, I do, and it eats girls,' Angus said and pulled a face. 'But it only likes sweet ones so that means it won't eat you, Poppy.'

Clementine leapt to her friend's defence. 'That's not very nice, Angus! But at least it won't eat me either.'

'Yes it will,' Angus insisted.

Joshua had been standing beside Angus the whole time, and now he gave his friend a funny look. 'Do you *like* her?' he asked.

'No way!' Angus shook his head. 'She's a girl and I don't like any girls.' Angus ran off into the playground with Joshua hot on his heels.

Astrid walked over to Poppy and Clementine. 'Angus *does* like you,' she said.

Clementine was confused by this comment. 'I don't think so. He's always so mean to me.'

'It's a boy thing,' Astrid explained. 'They're always mean to girls they like, so he probably likes you too, Poppy.'

Poppy pulled a face. 'Well, I don't like *him*, that's for sure.'

'I don't understand boys,' Clementine said seriously. But she was glad that Astrid did.

The day seemed to go by in a blink. Lady Clarissa picked Clementine up after school and when they got home the marquee was gone and there was hardly anything to remind Clemmie of the excitement of the weekend.

That evening, her mother helped pack her princess costume into a separate bag along with Angus's present, which Clementine took from the sideboard in the kitchen where it had been sitting next to Uncle Digby's.

Clementine took ages to fall asleep. She was so excited about the party and she couldn't wait for Uncle Digby to get home either.

Unlike Monday, Tuesday seemed to drag on for ever. Mrs Bottomley got cross with the children asking her what time it was over and over. She decided she might as well use their interest to have some lessons on reading a clock. Clementine thought that was long overdue. She'd been wanting to learn to tell the time ever since the first day.

When the bell finally rang, Mrs Bottomley supervized the children getting changed into their costumes. Much to Clementine's distaste, Mrs Bottomley made them form two straight lines to march the short distance to Angus's house. It was only around the corner from the school. They must have looked a strange lot in their crowns and robes, especially the children who were brandishing swords and sceptres.

The group was ushered out into the back garden.

'Hello Mr Smote,' Clementine cried, as she ran up to the man. He too was dressed as a king.

'Clementine!' He made a deep bow. 'How lovely to see you again.'

She glanced around the garden and saw a huge cardboard castle. It was big enough for the children to clamber into. There were shields hanging from the fence and even some wooden horses for the guests to be photographed riding.

'You really are a magician!' Clementine said.

'It was nothing much,' the man replied modestly. 'And Angus is such a good boy.'

Mr Smote definitely hadn't seen Angus at school, Clementine thought to herself.

Angus's mother and Mr Smote had arranged lots of games for the children to play. There was pass the parcel and pin the tail on the pony, musical statues and hide and seek. Clementine and her friends weren't as keen on that one, as Angus kept pointing out where he kept his dragon.

Astrid marched off to the bottom of the garden and hid right where Angus said the dragon had its lair. Clementine thought she was terribly brave.

The afternoon went very quickly. As the sun started to fade, Angus blew out the candles on his castle cake and the children gathered around to watch him open his presents. Some of the parents had started to arrive too.

Joshua had bought him a train set, Poppy had given him a superhero dress-up costume and Sophie gave him a football.

Clementine's present was last of all. She and her mother had found him a tiny remote-controlled bug that could actually fly. Clementine would like to have kept it for herself but her mother said that it would make a lovely gift for a six-year-old boy.

The children stood around watching and waiting as Angus tore open the paper. Clementine looked at the little brown box. Her heart sank.

Angus pulled off the lid and stared. For a moment he didn't say a thing. Clementine was about to speak but Angus got in first.

'Wow!' he gasped. 'That's the best present ever.'

Clementine gulped. 'But it's the wrong one.'

'What do you mean?' Angus looked at her with a frown.

'That's not yours.' Clementine's lip trembled and tears prickled the backs of her eyes.

'But it's cool,' Angus said, 'and it's mine now.' He gently lifted the shell from the box. 'Whoa, what is it?'

Mrs Bottomley leaned in and inspected the gift. 'That is a very rare and precious cicada shell,' she informed the wide-eyed onlookers.

'It's the best present ever.' Angus was so excited he turned and kissed Clementine's cheek.

Everyone giggled and Clemmie's cheeks flushed pink.

Angus's ears turned bright red.

'Gross! Girl germs,' Joshua called out.

A hand reached through the crowd and Mrs Tribble yanked her son by her side. She scooped him up and kissed him noisily on the cheek too. 'I'll give you girl germs, Joshua Tribble.'

Joshua's howls of protest had everyone in stitches.

'Don't worry, Clementine,' came a voice beside her. It was Aunt Violet. 'Pertwhistle will understand.'

Clemmie glanced up, surprised. She hadn't noticed her great-aunt arrive. 'Do you really think so?'

Aunt Violet winked. 'I know so.'

It was time to go. The children said goodbye and Angus handed out the lolly bags. When he gave Clementine hers he even said another special thankyou and gave her a hug. Clementine kept her hands by her side as he squeezed her extra tight.

'I love it,' Angus whispered.

'Come along, Clemmie,' her great-aunt instructed. 'Your mother and Uncle Digby should be home by now.'

'Uncle Digby,' Clementine yelled as she ran ahead of her great-aunt into the house. Uncle

Digby was sitting at the kitchen table sipping a cup of tea and looking his usual self again.

He grinned at her. 'Hello there, miss.'

Clementine raced around and gave the old man a tight squeeze. 'We missed you so much. And Mummy and Aunt Violet and Mrs Mogg had to run the whole wedding and it was almost a disaster when the hot water broke but then Aunt Violet fixed it,' she babbled. 'Is your heart better?'

'My old ticker is just fine. Nothing to worry about,' he replied.

She was glad to hear it. It seemed that Arya was right about her father being able to fix broken hearts.

Clementine released Uncle Digby and rushed over to the sideboard. Uncle Digby's card was there with Angus's present. She picked up the card and took it over to the table.

Aunt Violet motioned at the little box. 'Go on, Clementine, give Uncle Digby his present too,' she said.

'But . . .' Clementine began.

'But nothing, Clementine. It's the thought that counts,' her great-aunt encouraged her.

Clemmie raced back and picked up the parcel. She looked with sad eyes at the old man. 'I wanted this to be perfect.'

Uncle Digby studied the card. On the front was a picture of Clementine and Lavender standing beside Aunt Violet and Pharaoh and Lady Clarissa. It said: 'What's missing?'

He opened it up and inside there was a picture of himself.

'You', it said. A tear formed in the corner of his eye. He brushed it away hastily and then read the message aloud. Clementine had told her mother what she wanted to say and then copied it carefully into the card after her mother had written it on a piece of paper.

Dear Uncle Digby, get well soon. We miss you so much – even Aunt Violet. Lots of love, Clementine and Lavender xxx

Uncle Digby laughed. So did Lady Clarissa, and even Aunt Violet managed to smile.

'Well, aren't you going to open your present?' Aunt Violet asked.

Digby Pertwhistle picked at the sticky tape and then unwrapped the paper. Clementine stood beside him as he lifted the lid off the box.

'Oh!' he exclaimed. 'I've wanted one of these since I was a boy.'

'Really?' Clementine grinned. 'Is that true?'

Aunt Violet coughed. 'They didn't make them a hundred years ago, Pertwhistle.'

He pulled out the remote-controlled bug, which closely resembled a giant bumblebee, and the little controller that went with it.

'Let's give it a whirl.' He flicked the switch. The tiny wings began to flap. The insect took off, whizzing through the air and dive-bombing Aunt Violet.

'Steady on there, man,' she yelled.

His mouth twitched. 'Oh, we're going to have a lot of fun with this one.' He sent the bug flying past Lavender, who grunted loudly, and Pharaoh, who swatted at it with his paw.

'Thank you, Clementine. It's perfect.' Uncle

Digby put his arm around her and kissed the top of her head just as the little bug crash-landed onto the table, right into the middle of one of Pierre's strawberry sponge cakes.

Clementine gave Uncle Digby a hug and then smiled at her mother and great-aunt. Yes, it was – just perfect.

CAST OF CHARACTERS

Clementine Rose Appleby	Five-year-old daughter of Lady Clarissa
Lavender	Clemmie's teacup pig
Lady Clarissa Appleby	Clementine's mother and the owner of Penberthy House
Digby Pertwhistle	Butler at Penberthy House
Aunt Violet Appleby	Clementine's grandfather's sister
Pharaoh	Aunt Violet's beloved sphynx cat

Friends and village folk

Margaret Mogg	Owner of the Penberthy Floss village shop
Clyde Mogg	Husband of Mrs Mogg
Father Bob	Village minister
Pierre Rousseau	Owner of Pierre's Patisserie in Highton Mill

School staff and students

Miss Arabella Critchley	Head teacher at Ellery Prep
Mrs Ethel Bottomley	Teacher at Ellery Prep
Sophie Rousseau	Clementine's best friend – also five years old
Poppy Bauer	Clementine's good friend – also five years old
Angus Archibald	Naughty kindergarten boy
Joshua Tribble	Friend of Angus's
Astrid	Clever kindergarten girl

Others

Mrs Tribble	Joshua's mother
Sebastian Smote	Wedding planner

Dr Brendan Gunalingam	Groom's brother
Karthika Gunalingam	Groom's sister-in-law
Arya, Alisha and Aksara Gunalingam	Groom's nieces and nephew
Ryan Gunalingam	Groom
Harriet Fox	Bride
Roberta and Hector Fox	Bride's parents
Uncle Orville Fox	Great-uncle of the bride

ABOUT
THE AUTHOR

Jacqueline Harvey taught for many years in girls' boarding schools. She is the author of the bestselling Alice-Miranda series and the Clementine Rose series, and was awarded Honour Book in the 2006 Australian CBC Awards for her picture book *The Sound of the Sea*. She now writes full-time and is working on more Alice-Miranda and Clementine Rose adventures.

www.jacquelineharvey.com.au

Look out for Clementine Rose's
other adventures!

CLEMENTINE ROSE
and the
Surprise Visitor

Jacqueline Harvey

Can Clementine solve the mystery of an unexpected guest?

CLEMENTINE ROSE

and the
Pet Day Disaster

Jacqueline Harvey

Clementine can't wait for her school's special Pet Day.
Will she win a prize?

CLEMENTINE ROSE
and the
Farm Fiasco

Jacqueline
Harvey

Can Clementine save her class trip from disaster?